The Dark Goddess

The Dark Goddess

RICHARD S. SHAVER

ÆGYPAN PRESS

From *Imagination Stories of Science and Fantasy,* February, 1953.

Special thanks to Greg Weeks, Mary Meehan, and the Online
Distributed Proofreading Team (which can be found at
http://www.pgdp.net).

The Dark Goddess
A publication of
ÆGYPAN PRESS

www.aegypan.com

Deep within her caverns the great mer-woman longed for death to end her loneliness. But then came a voyager from space — a man — also lonely. . . .

*T*he black-emerald water swirled and broke in many silver gleamings. From the misty center of the pool rose a vast but beautiful head. The long dripping hair was not hair, but had a rippling life of its own. The great lonely eyes and wide scarlet mouth were far more lovely than any human's. The gleaming green shoulders and shapely long arms ended in graceful webbed fingers. The red tipped breasts were proud, naked mounts where beauty lived forever. The pillaring waist — the strong-arched hips that did not divide into legs but into two great serpentine drivers — ended in the wide tail fins of a fish.

The dark sea-scented lapping green water was circled by tiers of marble seats, where many human people sat, their eyes upon the throne-seat into which the tremendous female figure vaulted in one powerful thrust from the water, as a tall wave uncurls effortlessly upon a golden beach.

The people bowed their heads and waited for her words, and she sat for a long time looking on them sadly and somehow conveying that they had long disappointed her. When her voice came, a great bell of meaning in the sea-cavern, the humans began to weep, for they knew now in their hearts they had failed her.

"My people, when the first of you came here I welcomed you. I was glad, for I had been long alone. I never knew my own origin, my own race, and the wisdom that I learned here in these caverns I was glad to give to the young and ignorant voyagers that first came.

"An age ago, before any of you saw life, the work began. Today, this home of ours is the fruit of long labor, of generations of men. We do not like to give up our home, built to house our genius, to provide everlasting protection against the unstable elements."

Her people, of several shapes and sizes, sourcing from an amalgam of many human races of divergent strains from several near-forgotten planets, all sighed together, like a little wind of sadness. And something about that resignation of theirs seemed to anger the great green mer-woman's eyes, but her voice did not reflect that anger. All about them, below and above and on and on around the ancient bedrock of the dark planet, tier on tier and level on level, their cavern city stretched, a myriad homes for a myriad individuals.

"Today we face a contingency long foreseen. One which we hoped time itself would change, through some new force changing the motions of those bodies which circle ahead of us in space. It was foretold that in time this planet in its free course through space would be attracted to one or the other of two great suns which it will pass — or encounter. It is most probable that our planet will find an orbit about one of those suns ahead.

"Today that fate is no longer a prediction from an astronomer peering into far space. It is a fact we face within short weeks, not in some far future time. Already the surface ice is melting, seas forming above.

Already those who used to travel on the surface on their duties and observations have been affected by the powerful radiations of those suns. Those radiations when we are caught and held close will shorten the life span to a hundredth of what it is now. You must go, and go now. You must seek out a new home in the darkness of space where no sun shines to cut your lives short."

A low sob broke from the almost silent people; then another. For years they had known this would occur, but now there was no time left. It was hard to think of leaving their ancient home. A low and youthful voice asked, a clear ringing voice:

"And what of you, Alfreya? How can you accompany us? There has been no ship built to hold the water you must have, no ship great enough to hold your weight or lift it. What will you do?"

Her laugh was somehow one of vast relief, of humor of some mysterious kind they could not fathom, of loneliness glad once more to be alone. "I remain. This is my home, and if my knowledge is not great enough to fight off the death the new sun brings then I will welcome death. It could be, dear people, that I am weary of life."

The people could not hear her inward thought — "and of other lives, too . . ." — but perhaps they felt it in their hearts.

The gigantic mer-creature dove then, from her throne into the green-dark water, and left her people to their own devices. They saw her no more.

*T*he evacuation under way, the great ships lanced upward, one after another. One every three seconds, for a month of earth time. And deep in the water of her subterranean abode, it seemed to one great heart that with each blast of sound as another great ship lifted, some weight lifted from her heart.

The people of the Dark Goddess leaving their ancient home were very numerous, and very sad. But few of them thought twice of their ancient benefactress who had welcomed their ancestors, taught them, started them abuilding in the rock their vast cavern homes. If she wished to remain and die, that was her affair. She was not human. She was only a bit of ancient history that had somehow remained alive.

All of the people of the dark planet of ice were included in that migration. Not one remained to face death with their ancient Goddess. The dark planet moved on into its new orbit, empty of life. Empty, that is, except for one dark lonely heart. The mer-creature was too vast of body for any ship to hold. Besides, she breathed water — and she did not want to go. That was very strange. Very strange indeed. Of all that myriad of departing voyagers, not one understood why their Dark Goddess did not wish to go along. Which perhaps explains the mystery.

*A*n age passed. Or was it but a few years, a hundred or so? The mer-woman did not count the years. The once free planet now circled the angry red sun as a humble captive. On its now warm surface soil formed and plants grew. Trees and animals began to move about, grow larger. It was a new wild jungle planet, untouched by organized intelligence of any kind.

Deep down in the dim caverns, in her deepest lair, the mistress of an age of magic slept, and waked, and slept again. And what she thought about, and what she waited for, and what she did with the endless time on her hands, were mysteries. Mysteries, at times, even to herself. But her heart was sometimes very light, and glad to be alone, and at other times, very sad, and very sure that mankind itself was not what she would wish it to be. In searching her heart, Alfreya knew she was very well rid of all that clutter in the caverns overhead.

*F*rom the outer darkness of space came a tiny shape, speeding on and on toward this sun and captive planet. It was going from nowhere to nowhere at a terrific rate.

There are many shapes adrift in space, bits of rock, celestial debris awash in the infinite oceans of ether. But this shape was not a rock. It was of metal, and within it was a man named Peter McCarthy.

He was a very hungry man, and a very thirsty man, and when the great red sun reached out and pulled his ship to itself, Pete in his fuel depleted craft gave silent thanks that at last the end had come.

This would be a quick clean death in the flames, and Pete turned his back on the sun and waited. But when he heard the air screaming about his hull, he turned back to the bow view panes again.

"Well, I'll be damned!" cried Peter McCarthy. For a huge green planet had pushed itself between him and the sun, and he did not like that at all. "It's another of cruel Fate's devices to lengthen my torments!" said Peter, and wept salt tears of weakness.

But his hands responded automatically. They thrust to the controls in front of him and fired the long unused jets. A bit of fuel had collected in the bottom of his tanks, and the jets blasted out, the ship lifted, held itself upright on a pillar of sudden flame. Pete let it sink, swiftly but gently, so that it fell hissing into the rolling green seas without smashing to bits.

It sank down through the green waters like a stone, and McCarthy fell weakly across the controls, and did not move a finger to change her downward course. In truth, he hoped the ship would never come up again. He was sick and tired of fighting against death.

Hours passed, and he slept, dreaming vague little dreams of eating and drinking and flirting with the girls in the streets of Port Freedom. No light came through the single hemisphere of transparence in front of his nose, and he finally switched on the search-beam on the ship's nose.

"Stuck in the mud, I hope, jade that she is, and good for her, making me die like this," Pete muttered, hating even the cracked crazy sound of his own voice.

But the bowlight shafted ahead in brilliant clarity, piercing no ocean depths or ooze or mud-flats, but glancing over the racing ripples of a flowing river. Above the river surface the rocks came down, so low Pete could hear them touch the hull, scrape, grind free, as their touch sent the craft deeper in the hurrying water.

"Holy old Harry," growled McCarthy, rubbing at his slackened features. "She fell right through the bottom of the sea into some subterranean flow. . . ." He yawned, and stretched a little, and cursed again. "Sure, I couldn't expect her to do anything else, with my luck aboard her. There were trees and sunlight, and water . . . ah, water . . . up there, somewhere. I saw them, falling in, I did. Do I land where I can get anything like water? Hell no! I crash right on down into this hole!" He laughed a weak bitter laugh. Then he leaned back and began to sing through cracked and bleeding lips:

"There's a hole in the bottom of the sea;
There's a rock in a hole in the bottom of the sea;

There's a crab on a rock in the hole in the bottom. . . ."

And he began to snore, having fallen asleep.

Some hours later, Peter McCarthy awoke, little refreshed because of the raging thirst within him. With terrific effort he got to his feet, noting that the ship was no longer moving.

The bow light was still burning, but it showed only a black wall of smooth rock ahead. He switched it off, turning on the inside lights. He staggered and cursed his weakness, but he made it to the airlock. With feeble hands he tugged the little wheel around that pulled back the big bars on the lock door.

"I'll get this over with, somehow. I'll just jump into the damned black water and drink the damn river dry. . . ."

The big outer lock door swung open, and he straightened, half expecting a rush of icy water about his feet. But instead a warm and slightly fragrant air drifted silently in, touched his tangled hair with idle and somehow playful fingers.

"Still teasing me, you dirty old tramp!" growled the lean McCarthy, to whom death had become a personal enemy, a figure he had both pursued and fled from across a vast and empty space. A nemesis he could not escape, and a fiend he could not quite catch.

He tugged loose a hand flash from the bracket by the lock, and staggered out upon the smooth rock floor against which the ship had come to rest. He snapped on the light, and then he stood gaping stupidly at the rock walls in disbelief.

There were carvings, deep cut reliefs of utter beauty, twining vine leaves, little figures half-human peeping from the leaves, lovely female bodies as the flowers, incredibly lovely female heads in clusters as the fruit.

"I've come to the Halls of Bacchus himself! Sure, I must be dead already. No wonder I can't manage to die! But if that ain't the vine itself, I've never been drunk!" Pete was half delirious, half in the darkness of utter despair. But his Irish heart whispered to him, "Where there's the vine there's wine," and he tottered off weakly into the dark in search of it.

Somewhere afar off he heard a faint mysterious laugh, strangely feminine, strangely friendly. He stopped, for ahead of him was approaching a strange faint light. Closer it came, stalking toward him fearfully, and to anyone else it would have seemed like an animated clothing store dummy without the clothes. But the figure was feminine, and it bore on its shoulder a tall oval vaselike vessel.

Pete straightened, and awe swept over him. In a low voice he heard himself quoting —

"Came toward me through the dusk an angel-shape,
  Bearing on her shoulder a vessel . . .
  And bid me taste of it. 'Twas the grape!"

McCarthy's tongue twisted strangely in his mouth with a desirous life of its own. The glowing angel-shape bent, and held the vessel to his lips, and he drank long and deep. He wiped his mouth on the back of his hand, and looked into the angel's glowing eyes.

As he looked the shape changed, subtly, adapting itself to his approval like a dream might, and McCarthy whispered in an awed voice:

"Sure, lady, it is the grape right enough! Now tell me, are you the same angel who gave drink to Omar? Or was she your sister, maybe?"

The glowing shape, growing second by second more sweetly curved to his eye, unsmilingly replaced the vessel on her shoulder. Her voice was a distant melody though her face was right before his eyes:

"I am but a messenger, dear welcome stranger. I bid you consider these ancient halls your home. When you are well and strong, there will be many things to talk of, for I have been long alone. Mine eyes are glad with the sight of you."

McCarthy touched the naked angel's shoulder, and was surprised to find it hard as steel. The glowing being did not seem surprised, and her arm went about his shoulders, supporting him easily. After a minute of this slow progress, she bent and picked McCarthy up in her arms as if he were a babe. McCarthy murmured, "Sure angel, be this Heaven or Hell I'm damned glad to get here."

*T*he voyager lay unconscious for many days. While he slept, dozens of the weird "angels" hovered over him and what they poured down his throat and what they injected into his veins he never knew. But when at last he awakened he felt like the man he had been twenty years before, young in heart and with a boundless happiness of well-being surging up in him like a great spring of Omar's wine.

So waking, he sprang to his feet as he had used to do in the morning, unable to wait to learn what new and curious thing the day would bear for him. He looked about him with eyes that could not believe, and he was a long time remembering how he had got here or where he was. And when he did, it was to wonder why he had been so sunk in despair and so ready to accept death.

One of the tall glowing shapes came and bowed low before him, and McCarthy saw for an instant she was not a living woman at all, nor any angel either!

"Why you're a robot kind of thing!" cried Pete, recoiling in sudden distrust, for there was something revolting to him about a metal machine masquerading as a human form.

The glowing woman-shape straightened proudly, and her long fiery eyes narrowed a little, and her voice like distant tinkling magic murmured softly, "Are you so very sure I am not alive, man from afar?"

McCarthy kept looking at her, and she changed before his very eyes, and at last his wits awoke, so that he said gallantly, "Sure and you're as beautiful a woman as ever I saw in my life! I'm owing you my life, and I'd be the last would want to hurt your feelings. Nobody could be sorrier for the mistake than I am."

Now whatever she was, he could no longer tell her from a living woman of great beauty, for she had changed before his eyes from a metallic monstrosity of glowing terror to a softly curved beauty that would have graced the stage of any musical show, and her voice was far too good for any show that Pete had ever listened to. As she moved closer to him, her weirdly lovely voice whispered, "So my arms are hard as steel, man from space?" and put her arms around him, and they were soft and firm and fine arms to feel indeed.

Peter McCarthy, in sudden wonder, kissed the glowing weird lips of the lovely thing, and the taste was different but far more lovely than any woman's lips had ever been before.

"Now may God strike me, but I must be losing my wits," swore McCarthy, "but I had thought you were made of steel for sure!"

Somewhere afar there came a music of laughter; he could not exactly hear it but he felt it, as if the very walls were amused with him. It was a powerful laugh, with an undertinkling to it, like a distant bell beneath water, struck by a little stone so that it gave out both strong sounds and little sounds. . . . A very beautiful laugh but very strange to hear.

With the sound of that laughter an awe came to McCarthy; he felt the touch of some terrific magic, and he gave up trying to understand what was happening to him.

"This is a strange place," he muttered, rubbing his chin. "A strange place indeed. Could ye tell me, Miss Angel, what place this is and how I can expect to get along here and why you're so good to a poor wanderer like myself?"

The angel-shape — which second by second was getting to be more and more the shape of ultimate beauty to his eye, as if she was learning the way of it better and better right out of his mind, as if she was taking from his own thinking the colors and the shapes and form and spirit that would please him most — gave a laugh that was very like the strange great tinkling sound from nowhere. Her voice was like sparkling water falling on suspended crystals that rang musically, and she looked into his eyes out of her own fiery strange eyes of terrible beauty.

"This is the best of all possible places you could have come to, and your host is the best of all possible hosts and what more do you need to know today, Peter McCarthy?"

For an instant a shadow passed over the strange glowing eyes of the angel-shape, as if she remembered something she did not want to remember, and he asked:

"What is that shadow of trouble, if this is so good a place for me?"

She answered him quickly as the shadow passed from her eyes: "That shadow is the future, which will eventually get into even this stronghold and end it all. But until that day comes, why you at least can make merry. And I will help you. . . ."

*S*o time passed. The visitor was very happy, living in a paradise of wonder and sensation and love such as no man of earth ever had before.

The days of McCarthy's dreaming became many. There were always about him several of the lovely glowing woman-shapes. Their forms were soft and seemed to become almost too perfectly what he most wished they would become, even as he looked and his mind tried to find imperfection, he found only perfection. It was opposite from earth-style love, where one ignores imperfections to think about the better parts and points of the loved one . . . where love is a slow schooling in seeing only the finest facets of one's chosen. Here, he could find no imperfections to ignore, and he had only to imagine some perfection to see it before him.

McCarthy could not consciously know that the heavenly looks of these lovely things was magic, but he had his suspicions, and was always turning around quickly to catch one of them off guard and looking like something other than the featured actress in an extravagant and too-undressed musical comedy. But he never succeeded, and always when he turned quickly he heard the far faint tinkle of bell-like laughter, and that tinkle was somehow not a tinkle, but a deep melodious chime so far away that it was broken into smaller sound by the echo.

"Somebody gets a big kick out of me," grinned McCarthy, and forgot about it. They waited on him hand and foot; every whim that came into his mind they gratified as soon as it was born. Food of the most exotic kind was set before him whenever he was hungry. When he wanted love, they gave him from a boundless store; though not love such as he knew about. It was instead an ecstacy of an intense and vibrant kind, an overwhelming flame that hovered always about the sweetly glowing bodies of them, a flame that was not anything but the essence of all desires, distilled and intensified by some strong but subtle magic.

But after a while it was his sleeping that McCarthy liked the most. For then dreams came visibly into his chambers, and before his mind's eye waved immense phantasmagorial adventures. When one of these adventures caught his fancy it picked him up like a womanish whirlwind of strangely soft dark arms and he became for the time of his sleep a God, to whom all things were possible and each tiniest part of these dreams was like a flower of unearthly and utterly exquisite beauty.

It was nearly a year by McCarthy's careless reckoning before he determined what was true and what was mere pleasant fantasy in his life.

That was a black day.

He awoke to find his chambers empty. No glowing heavenly shapes to wash him and dress him and caress him. No sweet laughter in his ears, and no light anywhere but what he made with his almost depleted hand flash.

*L*ike a man bereft of reason he rushed away through the endless vaulted cavern halls, seeking, seeking his loved playmates, his glowing angel-shapes. And his heart seemed about to burst in his breast with the terrible sense of loss, like a man who has just lost his family . . . and who thinks he will find them alive if he runs fast enough.

After an endless time of running and walking and panting his hand flash went dark in his hand and he flung it away. He went on like a madman, blind, caroming off the carved stone walls and on and on until at last he sank to the floor in exhaustion.

Lying there, in despair as dark as the utter darkness of the caverns, his eyes began to note after a time a soft glow spreading out before him. Still longer he lay, looking, and his eyes began to see that it was water glowing, rippling softly away before his eyes. The glow strengthened little by little, until he could make out a vast thronelike chair afar above the glowing water.

For a still longer time McCarthy did not believe his eyes, for on the throne was a mighty female figure of dark green flesh.

Her long dripping hair was not hair, but writhed softly about her beautiful head with a life of its own. The great eyes and wide scarlet mouth were not exactly human, but they were very attractive and kind and somehow lonely with a weight of wisdom. The gleaming shoulders and tremendous long arms ended in wide-webbed fingers. The red tipped breasts, the pillaring waist, the proud arched hips that did not divide into legs but into two great serpentine drivers finned and scaled like the tails of beautiful fish . . . were to McCarthy after all his dreams but figments of his overworked imagination.

Peter McCarthy lay silently looking on this new phantasm, wondering if he were still sane, and indeed, if he were still alive, or if this were perhaps a place into which a soul wandered after death — where nothing was as a man expected it to be. And in the midst of his wondering the great lovely sea-woman's head turned. Her eyes sought him out and that unearthly music of her voice murmured — a sound like the surf breaking on ringing rocks far off.

"You had to know the truth some time, Peter McCarthy."

Pete struggled to his feet and found his strength flowing back. And being the kind of man he was he plunged into the dark pool of cool water and swam toward the great throne. It was much farther than it seemed, and when at last he got there he found the throne was as tall as an office building in the great cities of earth, and the lovely mer-woman's body as mighty as a Titan of earth's misty dawn. Big she was, and just as beautiful close up as from the far shore of her pool.

McCarthy sat on the first step of the throne, at her wide fin that was not a foot at all, and looked up into her lovely tragic eyes, his heart pounding in his breast.

"Sure, sea-mother, I know now! You are the only living creature in all these vast halls, and all the lovely things you have been doing to entertain me you do because you are lonely. Has it been fun to play with me like a toy, sorceress?"

One of the great finned hands of her fanned the air in a gesture of negation. "Not too much fun, McCarthy. But interesting, for I have never met a man of your race, so childlike and simple and so easily made to believe in my magic. And have you not enjoyed this year with me?"

"It is not that, sorceress. It is that my heart is snared here, like an ape in a cage and will never again be free. What kind of life can please me now? After this life you have shown me, how can I ever want to breathe common air again?"

Her laugh was like music under water, like bells ringing in the deeps of the sea. Her hand touched him lightly, and the touch was like lightning from heaven striking him with eternal love. And the thunder of that lightning pealed through all his being, thunder on thunder of vast meaning, and there was nothing from his dreams to compare with the beauty and the wonder of the simple touch of her hand.

McCarthy turned his face up to the vast woman-shape above him, the wonder of her touch shining from his eyes, so that she laughed again as she saw the effect upon him.

"If there had been more like you among my people, I would not be here alone," she murmured, like distant sorrowful music above him, her voice that was so much more than a voice. "But my people were sated with wonder and tired of love and weary with having too much. They went off and left me because I said I wanted to remain — to die. And my heart was sad, but something in me was very glad to be alone. Now I am glad that you are here! But I am afraid that there is no way you can leave now."

McCarthy stretched out at the foot of her throne, a grin on his square Irish face. "So, I can't get away again! Now that's the sorriest word I've heard for years. Sure I'm the unluckiest mortal that ever was born."

The dark goddess laughed again, and there was something of a sweet child in the bell-tones of her laugh, that died away in soft and softer echoes in the endless dark about them.

. . . Something of a shy child, who had never been loved, and found the idea infinitely amusing. Her voice became softer and more beautiful still, and McCarthy was endlessly happy to hear that laugh, for it said so much stronger than any words could — "You are welcome here, you sad Irishman." And her voice said, "And do you want your angel-shapes and their wine back again, or do you want some other thing I might create for you out of these forgotten energy converters?"

McCarthy grinned contentedly, and rubbed his roughened face against the smooth calf of her leg beside him. "D'ye think I should shave, goddess?"

The great beautiful face bent over and examined his Irish countenance, the rugged features and twinkling blue eyes and the red hearty cheeks of him. "Why, man-child, you are quite good-looking as you are!"

"And as for them angels and their wine," added McCarthy, "don't you know one look at you is worth a thousand angels? Can't you see in my mind and know . . . I forget, ye've been doing that for one solid year. Sure, you green angel you, why should a man want any other shape or sound or wine than yourself?"

So it was that some years later a great ship burst up from the seas of the lonely planet and on the terrific wings of a mysterious power shot silently away into the trackless void. And at the helm was a red-cheeked Irishman and the rest of the vast ship was filled with water and the goddess herself. All of it, that is, except the part where the three little McCarthys came out of the water to play with their dad every day.